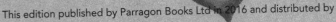

This edition published by Parragon Books Ltd in 2016 and distributed by

Parragon Inc.
440 Park Avenue South,13th Floor
New York,NY 10016
www.parragon.com

Copyright © Parragon Books Ltd 2004-2016

Written by Claire Freedman, Nick Ellsworth, Jillian Harker
Illustrated by Lorna Brown, Veronica Vasylenko, Kirsteen Harris-Jones,
Claire Henley, Caroline Jayne Church
Edited by Robyn Newton
Production by Jon Wakeham

ISBN 978-1-4723-1608-0

Printed in China

My
Ballerina
bag

PaRRagon

Bath • New York • Cologne • Melbourne • Delhi
Hong Kong • Shenzhen • Singapore

This book belongs to:

....

....

Contents

The Butterfly Ballerina

Isabella Ballerina loved ballet.

She liked twirling around in her pretty leotard.
She loved wearing her satin ballet shoes.

Best of all, she liked going to Madame Colette's Ballet School.

"Come, *mes petites*!" said Madame Colette—who was French and had once been a real ballerina. "Let us begin by warming up!"

The girls began their bending
and stretching exercises.

"Now, let us practice our ballet
positions!" said Madame Colette,
clapping her hands, as Miss Robin
played a beautiful tune on the piano.

"*Non, non,* Isabella!" cried Madame Colette. "You are pointing the wrong foot again!"

"Oops, sorry!" Isabella said. "I'm always getting my left and right muddled up!"

11

Isabella concentrated very hard, and the rest of the lesson went really well. She only turned the wrong way twice!

"*Bien!* Good!" said Madame Colette. "Wonderful pirouette, Isabella! Now, I have exciting news to announce!" Madame Colette told the girls that they would be putting on their very first ballet show.

"We will dance the Butterfly Ballet!" she said.
"This ballet is set in a beautiful flower garden. I
will choose girls to play raindrop butterflies, girls
to be rainbow butterflies, and one girl to dance the
beautiful sunshine butterfly!"

Back home, Isabella told Mommy all about the ballet. "Madame Colette says my ballet is getting better," she said. "I just wish I could remember my left from my right!"

"This might help my little Butterfly Ballerina!" Mommy smiled. She gave Isabella a beautiful butterfly bracelet. "Wear it on your right wrist; then you'll always be able to tell which way is right," Mommy told Isabella.

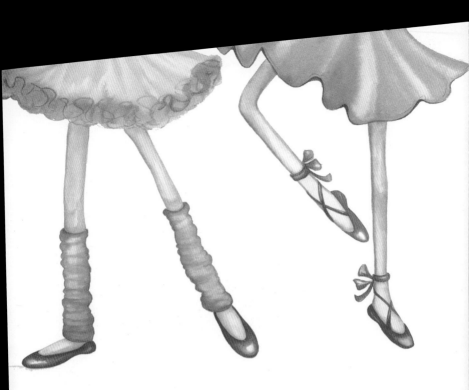

At each ballet lesson, the girls practiced their steps
for the Butterfly Ballet. Isabella kept looking down
at her butterfly bracelet to make sure she turned the
right way!

"*Non!*" cried Madame Colette as the girls twirled
around, pretending to be raindrop butterflies.
"Remember—you are gently falling raindrops—not
hailstones!" The girls giggled. They all tried to flutter
and spin gracefully.

16

Finally the decision time came, and Madame Colette told the girls, one by one, if they were going to be a raindrop or rainbow butterfly.

Soon only Isabella was left. "Oh no!" she thought. "I hope Madame Colette isn't leaving me out of the ballet because she's worried I might get my left and right mixed up!"

"Isabella, *ma petite!*" said Madame Colette.
"You shall play the sunshine butterfly. As you twirl
so beautifully, you will dance the final pirouette!"

Isabella just hoped she would turn the right way!

The week before the show, Isabella practiced her pirouettes everywhere! She twirled in the yard ... in her bedroom ... and at the park with her best friend, Hannah.

On the night of the big show, all the girls dressed in gorgeous tutus and delicate, shimmering butterfly wings. They tied matching ribbons in each other's hair. "Now we feel like real butterflies!" they giggled to each other.

Each girl's family was waiting in the audience. The lights dimmed. Miss Robin began to play the piano and beautiful music filled the room. The ballet was about to begin!

Out danced the raindrop butterflies, flitting
gracefully from flower to flower. Their sparkly silver
costumes twinkled in the soft lights.

Next, the colorful rainbow butterflies danced out,
linking arms before a beautiful arching rainbow.

At last it was Isabella's turn to dance. Nervously, she touched her butterfly bracelet.

Then she stepped
lightly onto the stage.

She fluttered to the middle, took a deep breath and twirled the most perfect pirouette she had ever twirled!

The girls joined Isabella on stage, and they all curtsied to the final tinkling notes of the music. Isabella smiled and touched her beautiful bracelet.

"Oops!" she giggled. She had curtsied with the wrong foot forward, but it didn't matter one little bit. She would always be Isabella, Butterfly Ballerina!

Ballerina's Magical Shoes

Lily the ballerina was hurrying to the theater. Today was the day of the grand ballet. Lily was dancing with her friends Wanda, Amber, and Tilly. They were all looking forward to dancing with Fleur.

Fleur was the Prima Ballerina and everyone loved her, especially Lily.

"Fleur is such a wonderful dancer," sighed Lily. "I wish that I could dance like her one day."

Fleur always danced in a magical pair of silver ballet shoes. Only the Prima Ballerina could wear them. They would not work properly if anyone else wore them.

They all loved to dance with Fleur, and watched her closely as she performed a perfect plié,

a beautiful arabesque,

and a stunning pirouette.

As the first dance ended, everyone clapped and the dancers followed Fleur off stage. They hurried to change their costumes for the next dance.

Suddenly, Fleur appeared in her bare feet, looking very upset.

"Something terrible has happened!" Fleur exclaimed. "I took off my silver ballet shoes to retie them and now they have gone. I won't be able to dance again until they are found."

"You mustn't worry," said Lily kindly. "We'll get them back for you."

"I'll look in the woods," said Wanda, hurrying out of the door.

"I'll look in the meadow," said Amber, as she ran off quickly.

"I'll look in the garden," said Tilly, dashing after her friends.

"We'll find the shoes in time for the next dance," Lily promised.

27

As Lily wondered which way she should go, she spotted a raven flying toward the woods. She could see something silver dangling from its beak.

"The silver shoes!" gasped Lily. "I'll have to run fast to keep up with that raven." And she ran after it.

Meanwhile, the ballet shoes grew too heavy for the raven.

They fell from its beak. The shoes dropped right in front of Wanda who was searching the woods.

"The magical shoes!" she said. "How beautiful they are. I'll just try them on quickly."

But as soon as Wanda put on the magical shoes, a strange thing happened. She danced a plié. She pliéd up and down and up and down, until she realized she couldn't stop.

"Help me, someone!" she cried, as she danced faster and faster.

Not far away, Lily could see her friend bobbing up and down in the distance. "I hope Wanda's all right," she thought, hurrying toward her. But poor Wanda pliéd out of the woods and into the meadow.

Wanda's legs were so tired she couldn't dance any more, and she fell flat on her back into a nearby bush.

"Are you all right?" asked Amber, who had been searching the meadow.

"Yes thanks," puffed Wanda. "But please help me take these shoes off."

Amber pulled off the magical ballet shoes and gazed at them. "They're so beautiful," she said. "I'm sure no one would mind if I tried them on quickly."

Amber tried on the magical shoes and she danced a perfect arabesque. "I never knew I could arabesque so well!" she thought. Then she did another, and another, until she realized that she couldn't stop.

"Help! I can't stop!" poor Amber called, as she danced out of the meadow and into the garden.

By this time, Lily had caught up with Wanda and helped her out of the bush.

"Where are Fleur's ballet shoes?" she asked.

"Amber tried them on, and now she can't stop dancing," puffed Wanda.

"Quick, we must follow her," cried Lily rushing off.

Amber was so dizzy from dancing that she ended up in the fountain, with a large splash. "Help me out of here, someone!" she shouted, splashing around. Luckily, Tilly was nearby and ran to help. But when she saw the silver shoes lying on the ground, she just couldn't resist putting them on.

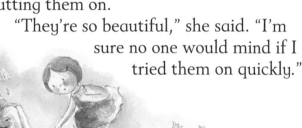

"They're so beautiful," she said. "I'm sure no one would mind if I tried them on quickly."

But when Tilly tried on the magical shoes, a strange thing happened.

She started to pirouette, around and around ...

"Wheee ... this is fun!" exclaimed Tilly. But then she began to spin faster and faster, and realized that she couldn't stop.

"I never knew I could pirouette so well!"

Lily and Wanda helped Amber out of the water. "Where are Fleur's ballet shoes?" asked Lily.

"Tilly put them on and now she can't stop dancing," replied Amber.

"We'd better follow her," said Lily, running on. Poor Tilly pirouetted down the hill and straight into a muddy puddle.

The others caught up with her and helped her up.

Lily carefully took the precious ballet shoes off Tilly's feet.

"They are so beautiful," said Lily, and she wanted to try them on too. But in her heart, she knew that there was only one person who was meant to wear them.

"Let's return the shoes to the Prima Ballerina," she said to the others. "She'll be so happy we found them."

"My shoes!" exclaimed Fleur when Lily and the others returned. "How can I ever thank you?"

Fleur gave Lily a silver charm in the shape of her silver ballet shoes. It looked just like them. "Thank you," said Lily gratefully. "I'll treasure it for ever!"

"Now we must finish the show," said Fleur, looking around at the girls. But Wanda, Amber, and Tilly were in such a mess they couldn't go back on stage.

"Oh, dear!" Fleur sighed. "You won't be able to dance looking like that." Then Fleur turned to Lily with a smile. "We will dance together."

Lily danced with the Prima Ballerina. They danced a plié, an arabesque, and a pirouette. And they danced so beautifully together that everyone clapped and cheered more than ever. The magical silver charm helped Lily to dance the most beautiful dance of her life.

"I'll remember this evening for ever and ever," thought Lily, as she walked to the front of the stage and took her final bow.

Ballerina Bella & the Lucky Locket

Bella was very excited. She was thinking about her new ballet class after school. But Bella's mind never stayed on one thing for long. She was pouring milk on her cereal when she saw something interesting through the kitchen window.

She saw a long stripy tail disappearing into the flowers at the end of the backyard. "What's that?" she asked.

"Mrs. Hunter's cat," replied Mom.

But Bella didn't think so. "I bet it's a wild animal that's escaped from the zoo," she said. And she jumped up to get a better look.

"Watch out!" called Mom. But it was too late. Bella had poured milk all over the kitchen floor.

"I hope you'll pay more attention in your ballet class," Mom told her.

"Of course I will," said Bella.

When Bella came out of school that afternoon, she called to her mom.

"Look at Ballerina Bella, Mom!" and she began to leap and twirl her way across the playground. "You see," she said, as she twirled right past her mom, "I know exactly how to concentrate hard." And she really meant it.

But it wasn't quite that easy. In class, Miss Ross, the ballet teacher, showed the girls the five ballet positions.

They started to copy her in first position, then second position.

Bella was thinking really hard about her feet. She was trying to make sure that her arms and her hands were just right. She was doing very well. Then suddenly ...

…Bella saw a huge spider hanging from the ceiling by a thread. It reminded her of swinging on the swing hanging from the tree in her yard. She closed her eyes and imagined herself going backward and forward.

"Bella!" called Miss Ross. Bella opened her eyes. Everyone else was in fifth position.

"Oh dear," sighed Bella. "I must pay attention."

The next week, Bella made up her mind that she would think about nothing but ballet for the whole class. She was sure she could do it.

Halfway through the lesson, the class began to practice pirouettes.

Bella liked pirouettes. She was becoming really good at them. Everything was going well. Then suddenly …

… Bella noticed the caretaker running past the window, shouting. His dog must have escaped again. It was always trying to run off.

Bella tried not to think about the dog. She thought about her pirouette. She thought it must be time to stop spinning. She stopped. "Bella!" called Miss Ross. Bella looked around. Everyone else was facing the front of the class.

"Oh dear," sighed Bella. "I really must pay more attention."

Each ballet lesson was the same. Just when Bella most needed to pay attention, something interesting would happen.

Miss Ross decided to have a talk with Bella.

"Bella," she began, "you do know that ballerinas have to pay attention ..." She didn't get any further.

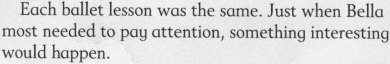

"What's that?" yelled Bella. "Is it a mouse? Look at its tail!"

The whole ballet class began to scream and run around.

"Oh, Bella!" sighed Miss Ross, as she picked up the piece of ribbon from the floor.

The time came for the class to rehearse their first show. Miss Ross reminded them that they all needed to pay extra special attention. She looked at Bella as she spoke.

As the girls danced, Bella noticed that Miss Ross wasn't always watching the girls. The teacher kept glancing around the room, as if she was looking for something. Bella and her friends began to dance. As they got close to the wings, Bella saw something interesting poking out from underneath the curtain.

The other girls started to move back across the stage. Bella disappeared off the stage.

"Bella!" called Miss Ross. "This is too much!"

"What's this?" asked Bella, running onto the stage with something shiny in her hands.

"You've found it!" smiled the teacher, taking the necklace from Bella and holding it up for all the class to see.

"This is the prize my ballet teacher gave to me when I was best dancer in my first show. It's a lucky locket. I wanted to give it to the best dancer tomorrow, but I thought I had lost it. Thank you, Bella. Where did you find it?"

But Bella didn't answer. Her eyes were closed. She saw herself on stage tomorrow, wearing the locket. She saw herself dancing better than she had ever danced in her life.

Bella kept this picture in her head. When she began to dance the following evening, she imagined herself dancing without making a single mistake. But it wasn't a dream. Bella did dance perfectly.

And when she stepped to the front of the stage to take her bow as the best ballerina, the lucky locket was sparkling around her neck.

Little Ballerinas

From the moment that Emily watched her first ballet, she knew what she wanted to be.

The ballet was "Sleeping Beauty". Emily loved the beautiful costumes, the wonderful music, and the pretty colored lights. But, above all, she loved the Prima Ballerina.

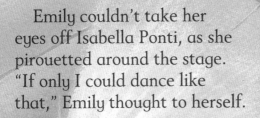

Emily couldn't take her eyes off Isabella Ponti, as she pirouetted around the stage. "If only I could dance like that," Emily thought to herself.

Emily was telling her best friend Hannah all about the ballet the next day, when her mom came into the bedroom.

"I have a surprise for you, Emily," said Mom. "I've arranged for you to have some ballet lessons."

Emily jumped up and down on her bed with excitement. "Wow!" said Hannah. "You're so lucky!"

"It would be perfect if you could come too," said Emily, hugging her friend. "Let's ask your mom."

Hannah's mom agreed, and their first lesson was arranged for next week. On Saturday, the two girls set out to buy their ballet clothes.

As soon as Emily put on her shoes, she started to do little jumps in the air. "These are sautés," smiled Emily. When she slipped into the pretty pink outfit, she felt like a princess. Around and around the shop Emily twirled.

"Watch me do a pirouette!" she called to Hannah and her mom.

"How do you know all these things?" asked Hannah.

"I've been reading about them," replied Emily, "and I can remember just how the Prima Ballerina did them."

The girls started their ballet classes the following week. While Hannah worried about each new move, Emily was the quickest to do everything in class.

Whenever their teacher showed them a new step, Emily could do it at once. She could perform a perfect plié ...
hold fifth position ...
and do a beautiful glissé.

Hannah tried really hard, but she found all the new steps so difficult.

51

One day, Emily and Hannah arrived at their lesson to find everyone already dancing. "We're not late, are we?" asked Emily.

"Haven't you heard?" said an older girl. "Isabella Ponti is coming to visit. Isn't it brilliant?"

"No wonder everyone's practicing so hard," said Emily, grabbing her friend's hand. "Come on, Hannah!"

When Isabella Ponti arrived, the excitement grew. The Prima Ballerina explained that she was looking for two girls to dance with her in a performance. She showed the class the steps she wanted them to practice. Everyone gasped when Isabella danced a beautiful arabesque. None of them had ever tried a pose like that.

Isabella asked the girls to choose partners. "I'll be back in a few weeks to choose one pair of girls to dance with me," she told them.

Lots of girls wanted to choose Emily as their partner, but no one wanted to dance with Hannah.

Emily thanked the others. "Hannah's going to be my partner," she explained. "She's my best friend."

"Are you sure?" whispered one of the girls.

"I wouldn't want to dance with anyone else," replied Emily.

Later in the park, Emily and Hannah talked about Isabella Ponti's visit. "I'm nowhere near as good a dancer as you," said Hannah. "You won't be chosen with me as a partner, and you deserve to be. You see, I feel so dizzy when I try to pirouette."

"Are you dizzy right now?" asked Emily, as the pair spun around on the grass.

"Not really," replied Hannah, puzzled.

"Well, you're going around and around," Emily told her. And she made Hannah dance a pirouette right there.

55

"But I wobble if I try to balance," insisted Hannah.

"Follow me!" yelled Emily, running along the park wall. "You see! You can balance when you don't think about it." And she made her friend do an arabesque right there.

"The most important thing to remember is that dancing is fun," Emily said to her friend.

By the end of that week, Hannah started to believe what Emily had told her. The two friends practiced together every day, and Emily made sure they shared lots of laughs.

On the day of the Prima Ballerina's visit, each pair showed her what they could do. At last it was Emily's and Hannah's turn to dance.

When Emily smiled at her, Hannah thought of all the fun they'd had … and she smiled back. She gave the biggest smile of all when they danced an arabesque together.

Isabella Ponti congratulated all the girls on their hard work. "You all performed really well," she said, "so you haven't made my choice easy. But one pair of dancers stands out—they work together, they smile at each other, and they made me feel that they find dancing fun. I'm choosing Emily and Hannah."

Four weeks later, the night of the performance had finally arrived. As the two friends waited to go on stage, Isabella came out of her dressing room.

"I have something for each of you," she said, holding out two beautiful silver bracelets. Three pairs of ballet shoes dangled from each bracelet. "I hope this will remind you always of our special evening together."

"Oh, thank you!" gasped Emily.

"My bracelet will also remind me that you can do anything with the help of a true friend,"added Hannah.

"I agree!" said Emily, smiling.

The two girls danced onto the stage after the Prima Ballerina. They performed their steps in perfect time.

As Emily and Hannah jumped and twirled, their two bracelets glittered under the dazzling stage lights.

That evening, it wasn't only the girls' bracelets that sparkled. Just as bright were the smiles the little ballerinas gave each other as they danced—the smiles of true friends.

Pink Ribbons

Ellie Price had wanted to be a ballerina for as long as she could remember. She started ballet classes at Miss Pepper's School of Dance when she was just five years old, along with her best friend, Mia.

Mia had stopped going to ballet when she was nine, but Ellie loved it. She practiced hard, passed her ballet exams, and then, when she was 11, she got a place at Madame Rosa's Central Ballet School in the city. It was a dream come true!

"So you actually have to sleep there too?" asked Mia, as she watched her friend pack her suitcase.

"I'll have ballet lessons every morning and school work in the afternoons," Ellie explained. "Most of the students live there."

"But won't you be really nervous and homesick?" asked Mia. "I know I would."

Ellie laughed. "Well, yes, I am nervous," she admitted, "but I'm really excited too. It's what I've always wanted."

"I know, but I'll miss you so much," said Mia, jumping off the bed and giving Ellie a big hug.

"I'll miss you too," said Ellie, hugging her friend right back.

Ellie's mother drove Ellie to her new ballet school the following morning. "I'll come and pick you up on Friday evening," said Mom anxiously. "Are you sure you'll be all right?"

"Don't worry," said Ellie. "I'll be fine."

And Ellie was fine—at least at first. She loved the ballet school's light, airy practice studios with their huge mirrored walls. She loved her bedroom, which she shared with two other new students, Yoshiko and Chloe. And she loved being able to dance every single day.

At the end of the first week, the new students had a lesson with the famous Madame Rosa herself.

"I've heard she is very strict," whispered Chloe, as she put on her ballet shoes.

Yoshiko was warming up at the barre. "Yes," she agreed. "One of the older girls said that if you don't get something right, she shouts at you!"

"But she was really nice at the auditions," said Ellie.

"Well, we'll soon find out," muttered Chloe. "Here she comes!"

The door opened and Madame Rosa walked into the room. Her dark hair, streaked with white, was scraped back in a bun at the nape of her neck. As always, she was wearing a black leotard, a black skirt, and black tights. Madame Rosa looked at each of the girls in turn.

"*Bonjour, mes filles,*" she said finally, in a heavy French accent. "Good morning, girls!"

"Good morning, Madame Rosa," chorused the students.

"Now, you are here at my ballet school because you are good dancers. Some of you may even join a ballet company one day. But, I must tell you now," she continued sternly, "the road ahead is hard. You must have patience. You must have perseverance. And you must practice, practice, practice." At the repetition of each word, Madame Rosa thumped the floor with her foot.

"Now, to work!" she exclaimed. "Right hand on the barre! Plié! Plié in first position … in second position … now in third … Good! Now, fourth … and fifth!" Along with the rest of the students, Ellie bent her knees smoothly and rose up on her toes, working through each step and the five positions of her feet and arms.

Madame Rosa put the girls through their barre exercises for half an hour. Then they moved to the middle of the room for center work. Ellie danced well. Finally, Madame Rosa asked the girls to put on their pointe shoes with hard blocked toes. Ellie had been dancing en pointe for six months, but, during her first lesson with Madame Rosa, she couldn't stop wobbling.

"Ellie! Again!" called Madame Rosa. But it was no good. Ellie kept losing her balance. She was in tears of frustration by the end of the lesson.

"Never mind, Ellie," said Chloe, putting her arm around Ellie's shoulders. "You'll be better next week, you'll see." But Ellie was not better the following week. In fact, if anything, her dancing was much worse.

"Ellie! Lift your arm higher," shouted Madame Rosa. "Ellie! Turn out your leg more, please!"

Ellie began to dread her dance classes with Madame Rosa. At the weekends when she went home, Ellie spent most of the time in her bedroom, feeling miserable.

"I don't understand, Ellie," said Madame Rosa one Friday morning. "You were such a good dancer at the audition … maybe we were wrong about you …"

"I think it's my shoes," said Ellie desperately. "Maybe my shoes don't fit properly!"

"Show me," demanded Madame Rosa. Ellie took off her shoes and handed them to Madame Rosa.

"Mmmm," said Madame Rosa. "They don't look worn to me ... and a good dancer never blames her shoes," she added.

"Even so," she continued thoughtfully, "a new pair of ribbons could be just what you need ... Yes," she said, making up her mind. "There's a ballet store just around the corner. Ask the lady for some new ribbons, sew them to your shoes, and I'll see you at class next week." Ellie grabbed her things and raced out of the studio. She walked past a row of old-fashioned stores with small windows. The ballet store, called Pink Ribbons, was on a corner.

A bell jangled as Ellie pushed open the door.

"Oh," she breathed. "What a magical place!" The shop was packed with all kinds of dancewear, from tights and tutus to leg warmers and leotards. Behind the wooden counter were rows and rows of glass-fronted drawers filled with ballet shoes.

The walls were covered with posters of old ballet performances. Ellie saw a photograph of a graceful ballerina dancing the part of the swan in Swan Lake. She sighed, her eyes filling with tears. She'd never be good enough to be a great ballerina like the one in the picture.

"Can I help you, dear?" A kind-looking old lady was standing behind the counter.

"Oh, yes, please," said Ellie. "I've come for some ribbons for my ballet shoes. Madame Rosa sent me."

"Madame Rosa?" asked the old lady. Ellie nodded. "Well now, let me see ..." said the old lady, opening one of the drawers behind her. "Are you happy at the dance school, dear?" she asked.

"Oh yes, I am," said Ellie. "I mean ... I was," she stammered, and then, unable to hold back her tears any longer, she began to cry.

"There, there," said the old lady, going over to Ellie. "Take my handkerchief, then sit down, and tell me all about it." The old lady had such a kind voice, Ellie told her about the problems she had been having at Madame Rosa's Central Ballet School.

"It seemed so easy at Miss Pepper's," sobbed Ellie. "At Madame Rosa's, everyone is a much better dancer than me. I can't seem to dance any more!"

"Dry your eyes," said the old lady, "and cheer up! I think I have just the thing you need—some pink, magic ribbons to sew onto your shoes." She disappeared into the back of the shop.

"Here they are," she said, coming back, and she put a pair of long, pale pink ribbons into Ellie's hand.

"Magic ribbons," breathed Ellie, eyes shining. "Really?"

"Yes," said the old lady. "Sew them to your ballet shoes and you will be able to dance well again. Trust me. Will you promise me you'll do that?"

"Yes, I will," promised Ellie. "Thank you! Oh, thank you!"

"Go on then, dear," smiled the shopkeeper. "Hurry back to school, and good luck!"

Ellie wore the magic pink ribbons to Madame Rosa's ballet class the following week. She danced beautifully.

"Did you get some new ribbons, Ellie?" asked Madame Rosa.

"Yes," replied Ellie.

"Well they seem to have worked," declared Madame Rosa. "Good for you!"

Ellie's dancing got better and better, and she even began to look forward to her weekly lesson with Madame Rosa. "Oh, Mia," she told her friend excitedly over the telephone. "You'll never guess what! Madame Rosa has picked me to dance the lead role in the school's next performance. Will you come and see me dance?"

"Try and stop me!" said Mia.

Over the next few weeks, the girls practiced hard for their performance. Then, on the morning of the show, disaster struck! Ellie couldn't find her ballet shoes with the magic pink ribbons anywhere. "They must be here somewhere," said Chloe, helping Ellie search their bedroom. The girls searched high and low but they couldn't find them.

"They will turn up, Ellie, don't you worry," added Yoshiko. "You've got your spare shoes, haven't you?"

"It's not that," said Ellie. "I can only dance in the shoes with the pink ribbons. You don't understand!"

After her lessons, Ellie rushed out of school to the ballet store.

"Help me, please," she gasped breathlessly to the old lady. "The magic ribbons you gave me! I've lost them and I need them tonight. I've got the lead role. I have to dance well!"

"Calm down! You mustn't worry!" said the old lady. "The ribbons I gave you were not magic—not magic at all."

"Wh … what do you mean?" said Ellie, confused.

"You just needed confidence, that's all," said the old lady. "The ribbons gave you that, didn't they? You see—the magic was in your feet all along, I could tell!"

She chuckled. "I did the same thing for another young ballerina, many years ago. See, there's her photo on the wall, dancing the lead in Swan Lake. It's hard to imagine that she needed a little confidence when she was a young dancer like you, but she did."

"Who is it?" breathed Ellie. "What's her name?"

"Don't you recognize her?" asked the old woman, smiling. "It's Madame Rosa, your teacher! Now, hurry along, dear, or you'll be late for your performance."

Ellie dashed back to the ballet school. As she raced down the corridor towards her room, she ran straight into Madame Rosa.

"Why, Ellie, I was coming to find you!" said Madame Rosa. "Why are you rushing? Is everything all right?"

"It is now," said Ellie. "I've been talking to the lady at the ballet store. She said you got some magic ribbons there too, a long time ago … well, not so long ago," stammered Ellie, blushing.

"It's all right, Ellie," smiled Madame Rosa, interrupting. "I know what you mean. It is a special store, isn't it?" she added, her eyes twinkling.

"Now, I've found a pair of ballet shoes," she continued. "I believe they are yours?"

"Oh yes," said Ellie. "Thank you!"

"All right. Enjoy the performance tonight, Ellie. I am sure you will dance beautifully!"

And she did—even though she knew the pink ribbons weren't really magic. The old lady in the ballet store was right, and everyone in the audience (including Mia and Ellie's mom and dad) agreed—the lead ballerina danced so gracefully, she must have had magic in her feet.

Showy Zoe

Ballerina Zoe could
Leap high off the ground,
And land so very gracefully,
She'd barely make a sound!

But though she was so graceful,
It went right to her head.
Instead of practicing her steps,
She used to boast instead.

It made the other dancers cross.
"We're quite fed up with Zoe.
Why does she have to brag so much,
And be so proud and showy?"

One day, Zoe had some news.
"I've heard about a show.
There's going to be an audition.
I think we all should go!"

"I know that I will win a part.
Of that, you can be sure.
But you might get a little role,
If you would practice more."

The day of the audition came.
"I'll stretch and do some bends,
To warm up ready for the test,"
Said Zoe to her friends.

But as she stretched her tutu ripped.
The others heard it tear!
"What shall I do?" Zoe cried.
"I've nothing else to wear."

"Don't worry!" Dizzy Izzy cried,
"We'll dance around you.
Then no one else will ever see
The hole in your tutu!"

So Di and Izzy twirled about,
With Zoe in between.
Zoe was delighted.
"We make a splendid team!"

"Now each of us has won a part!
It's very plain to see.
Not only are you thoughtful friends—
You can dance as well as me!"

Shy Di

Ballerina Di was
As dainty as can be.
No other ballerina
Danced as daintily as she.

When she skipped with other girls,
Holding hands together,
They said she danced as lightly
As a cloud or floating feather!

One day, the teacher told the class,
"There's going to be a show.
I want to give the leading role
To dainty Di, you know."

"I'm far too shy!" protested Di,
"I'd really rather not.
Already, I feel nervous—
My tummy's in a knot!"

No matter what the others said,
Di firmly shook her head.
"I think the teacher ought to choose
Someone else instead!"

So Zoe got the leading part,
To nervous Di's relief
(though Di did feel a little
disappointed underneath!).

Everybody practiced hard,
To learn their ballet part.
Until the dancers knew at last
Every step by heart!

Finally, the first night came,
But then disaster struck.
Zoe fell and hurt her foot.
It really was bad luck!

"You can't dance the leading part.
Whatever shall we do?
Shy Di is the only one
Who knows the part like you!"

Shy Di looked at all her friends.
"I'll dance the part," she sighed.
"I can't let my friends down.
At least I will have tried!"

She trembled as the curtain rose,
But as the music played,
Di could not believe it!
"I just don't feel afraid!"

Di danced as she had never danced.
The crowd all called for more.
"What a dainty dancer!
She's a star, for sure!"

Dizzy Izzy

Izzy loves to ballet dance,
Like lots of little girls.
She practices her steps each day.
She spins and jumps and twirls!

Izzy likes the music,
And the pretty costumes, too.
But twirling is her favorite thing.
It's what she loves to do.

But though she twirls so beautifully,
She has a problem, too.
"I can't tell my left from right!
Whatever can I do?"

When all the ballerinas
Start dancing to the right,
Izzy dances to the left.
It happens every night!

"Watch where you are going!"
Cried Ballerina Di.
"You keep stepping on my toes,
When you go whirling by!"

Ballerina Zoe said,
"She really has to go.
Unless she learns her left and right,
She's going to spoil the show!"

"I give up!" poor Izzy sobbed,
And ran off then to hide.
"I wish I knew my left and right.
What can I do?" she cried.

"Don't be upset," said kindly Di.
"I know what to do
To help you solve the problem.
Just give me your right shoe."

She tied a bell onto the toe,
And fixed it with a stitch.
"Now, when you hear it tinkle,
You'll know which foot is which!"

"How wonderful!" cried Izzy,
Twirling to the right.
"Now I know which one is which,
I'd love to dance tonight!"

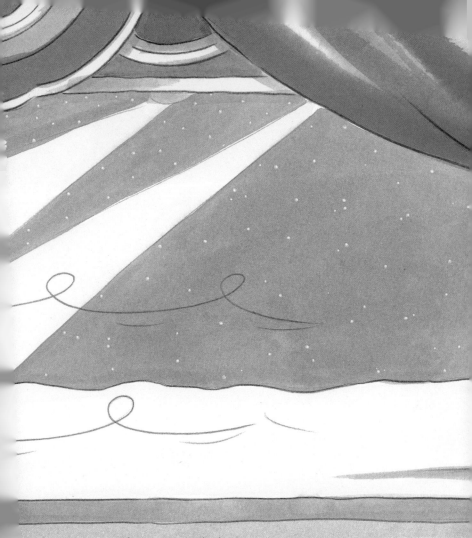

So Izzy wore her special shoe.
Her twirling stole the show!
"Now I can twirl up on the stage
And know which way to go!"